IMPISH THE ELF:
World Traveler

Amanda McIlwain Hauser

AuthorHouse™
1663 Liberty Drive
Bloomington, IN 47403
www.authorhouse.com
Phone: 1 (833) 262-8899

Because of the dynamic nature of the Internet, any web addresses or
links contained in this book may have changed since publication and
may no longer be valid. The views expressed in this work are solely those
of the author and do not necessarily reflect the views of the publisher,
and the publisher hereby disclaims any responsibility for them.

This book is printed on acid-free paper.

ISBN: 978-1-6655-0043-2 (sc)
ISBN: 978-1-6655-0042-5 (hc)
ISBN: 978-1-6655-0044-9 (e)

Library of Congress Control Number: 2020918048

Print information available on the last page.

Published by AuthorHouse 09/16/2020

authorHOUSE®

May the spirit of Christmas forever live in your hearts, precious family. Thank you for your unwavering support. Impish, the Hauser children will never forget the year you brought them an around-the-world Christmas experience. Thank you for keeping magic a part of every childhood!

For those who've not met her and may not know,

Santa's wrapping elf, Impish, found darkness her foe.

She simply detested a life dreary and bleak,

So she devised a plan of elfish hide-and-seek.

But at the top of the world, at the northernmost place,

The darkness long lingers and fills every space.

Cold hugs tightly to drifts of glass-like snow,

And winter makes camp with nowhere to go.

Yet light still burns in Santa's workshop up there,

From the bubbling, bright mind of this elf extraordinaire!

For years Impish toiled in winter's dark days,

Nimbly tucking and folding and taping away.

Clever and funny and sneaky and bright,

She invented a plot to bring forth joyous light—

A delightful and brilliant plan for her chums,

Twisted like peppermint, sweet like sugarplums.

Her expertly wrapped gifts came with no tags,

No names on the presents, the boxes, or bags.

And the children were left to solve her elf clues

That she left in their stockings for them to use.

Like many bright things that eventually fade,

Gray crept over the lightness Impish had made.

Neither cocoa nor cookies could bring her good cheer—

Nor sprinkles nor frosting nor chocolate reindeer!

Soon her fiery curls had lost all their spring,

And she hummed Christmas carols she would once boldly sing.

Alas, her wrapping tricks had run their full course,

So Impish's busy mind sought a new source

Of razzle-dazzling mischief she could prepare

To avoid feeling sadness and utter despair.

Now the jolliest elf took his daily rounds.

Yes, Santa himself checked the North Pole grounds.

He surveyed the workshop as timely as a clock,

Checking every department, down to each key and lock.

There he found his wrapping elf glum and a bit hunched

Over her elfish scribbled plans and a half-eaten lunch.

In no time flat, the merry man did spy

Impish lacked a glow and twinkle in her eye.

Curious, he tiptoed through the stained glass door,

Worried for li'l Impish, wanting to learn more.

It took a bit of prodding, but Santa's elf came clean.

She loved crafting surprises but had never really seen

The faces of those who discovered, on early Christmas Day,

The wrapping clues she had designed to enhance their holiday.

And her elfin sorrow Santa completely understood,

So he concocted a plan to help—one only Santa could!

"Join me, li'l Impish, on a magical midnight ride!

Hop upon the velvet sleigh seat; sit right by my side.

Let's visit those who've uncovered your brainy elfish ruse

Of presents without the nametags that you previously used."

The thought of an adventure brought light to her dull cheeks.

With a scarf around her neck and feeling warmer than in weeks,

Impish boarded, and she buckled up; she held on super tight.

Santa coaxed his reindeer, "Ho! Ho!" and glided through the night.

Continents and wide oceans, towering mountains and vast plains

Flashed silently below them as Santa pulled on the reins.

They saw the Serengeti, the Great Wall, the pyramids too,

The rainforest, Mount Everest, and there was Timbuktu;

The Eiffel Tower and grand Lady Liberty,

Big Ben itself, and the Opera House in Sydney.

Each wondrous destination marked on Santa's map—

Which lay like a quilt across Impish's lap—

Was a miracle, a gift, to the wrapping elf's heart,

As she spied children there who had each been a part

Of the tricks and the clues and the gifts she'd prepared

To bring light to the darkness, to show how she cared.

Their smiles told stories she never before knew.

She listened to their whispers; her joy slowly grew

To the top of her throat and out through her lips.

Ideas flashed through her brain like the crack of a whip!

"I've got it!" she yelped, and Santa jumped in his seat.

"Santa, my new plan—it simply cannot be beat!

The globe is a treasure we all must share;

My newest wrapping trick will make them aware

That some of our greatest gifts are found on this earth,

The lands of their friends, of their ancestors' birth.

Let's show them the riches from faraway places.

My clue of the year will light up their faces!

Back to the Pole, Santa—hurry up, go!

I have work to do, so much more than you know!"

Diving through the clouds near the great Taj Mahal,

The sleigh swooped west, past Niagara Falls,

Then banked to the north as Impish jotted her notes.

The polar winds whipped through their gloves and their coats.

A bit of a shiver landed them safely back.

Impish rushed to her desk; she had plans to unpack!

"Suitcases," she murmured with a head scratch and a scribble,

"World travelers will need them." A quick pencil nibble.

"Passports to lead them, destinations to show …

Which presents to open, which places to go."

A whirlwind followed, and Impish designed

All the parts and the pieces for children to find.

Clues for the stockings and presents unnamed—

The globe-trotting elf made a worldly game.

So on Christmas morning, we will travel the sphere,

Visit majestical places, the far and the near.

First, check the passport; it's stamped full of hints

To discover the presents that Santa has sent.

The world is a gift, Impish's magical muse.

Where will you travel? She left you the clues!

Author Description

Amanda McIlwain Hauser makes magical childhood experiences her mission. As a mother of eight children, an elementary teacher, and an author, Amanda spends most of her time creating ways to engage children. Keeping magic a part of childhood has always been her passion.

Growing up on a farm in rural Indiana, she spent her free time crafting, experimenting, creating, imagining, writing, and exploring, and those expressive threads have followed her through all seasons of life. Earning writing awards throughout her childhood, Amanda continued her education at St. Joseph's College in Rensselaer, Indiana, where she graduated valedictorian of her class with a degree in elementary education. She went on to earn her master of education degree in curriculum and instruction from Indiana Wesleyan University. After teaching nearly fifteen years in the public classroom, Amanda homeschooled her children with a self-created yearlong curriculum that immersed the family in various learning experiences across the United States.

But learning didn't end during holiday breaks for the Hausers! Impish has visited the family for nearly fifteen years, bringing challenges, clues, and riddles to encourage imagination, collaboration, and excitement on Christmas morning. But most of all, Impish's antics heighten the anticipation and magic children feel during this important time of year. In her first book, *Impish the Christmas Elf*, Amanda began sharing the tradition of the creative gift-wrapping elf with the world. In *Impish the Elf: World Traveler*, the second book of the Impish series, the world itself is Impish's clue of the year. Join Amanda and the Hauser family in this unforgettable Christmas gift-giving tradition!

To get enrichment activities, gift ideas, and inspiration from Impish herself, visit Impishtheelf.com under the blog tab!